ISLING

Cultural Ser es

This Little Tiger Book Belongs To:

_____

_____

_____

_____

For Toad, the dog with
the itchy back
~D.B.

For Bentley, our very
own shaggy dog
~G.W.

LITTLE TIGER PRESS
An imprint of Magi Publications
1 The Coda Centre, 189 Munster Road, London SW6 6AW
www.littletigerpress.com
This paperback edition published in 2001
First published in Great Britain 2001
Text © 2001 David Bedford
Illustrations © 2001 Gwyneth Williamson
David Bedford and Gwyneth Williamson have asserted their
rights to be identified as the author and illustrator of this work
under the Copyright, Designs and Patents Act, 1988.
Printed in Belgium • All rights reserved
ISBN 1 85430 737 1 • 3 5 7 9 10 8 6 4

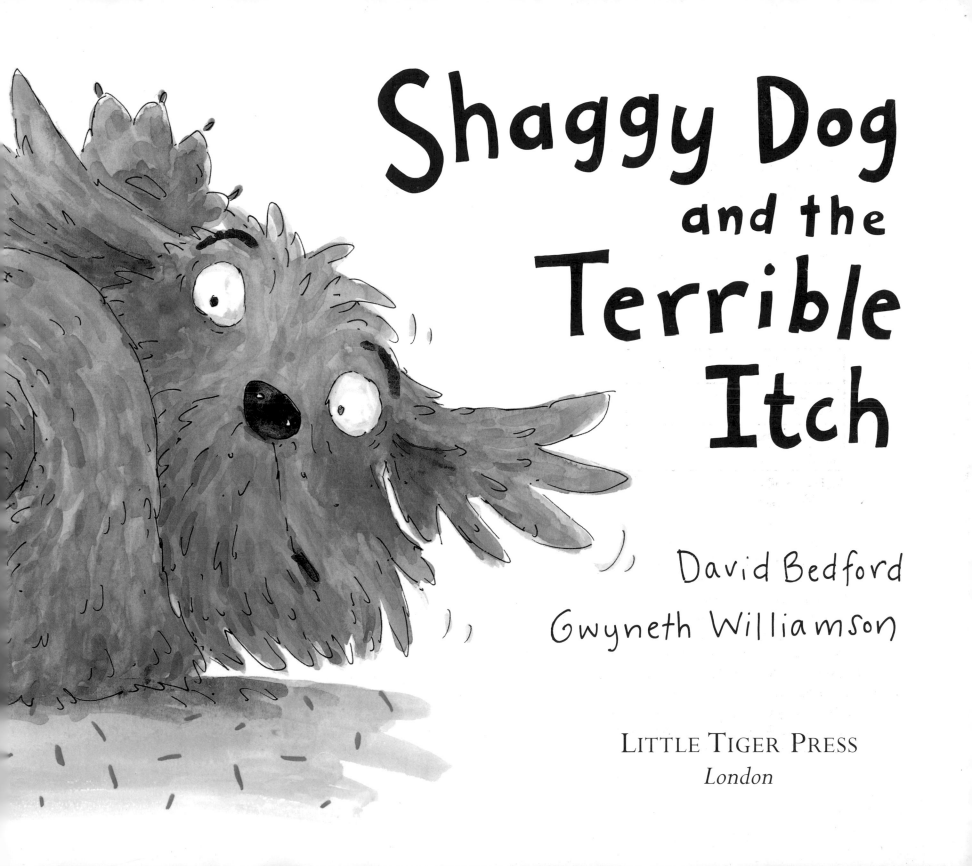

Shaggy Dog
and the
Terrible
Itch

David Bedford

Gwyneth Williamson

LITTLE TIGER PRESS
London

Shaggy Dog had an itch on his back.
He scratched against a tree but . . .

his back was still itchy.

"Will you scratch my back?"
Shaggy Dog asked Mimi the poodle.
"Ugh!" said Mimi, "scratch your
back, *no thank you!* I'm off to
the Poodle Parlour for a
wash and trim."

"*I* will scratch your back," said Farmer Gertie. "But first you must help me round up my sheep."

The sheep were hiding, and it took
ages to find them.
"*Woof woof!*" barked Shaggy Dog.
"Come here, sheep, come here *now*!"

At last the sheep were locked in their pen.
Farmer Gertie used her curly crook to scratch
Shaggy Dog's back.
"Ooh!" said Shaggy Dog. "That's much better."
But as Shaggy Dog walked into town . . .

the itch
came back!

Shaggy Dog knocked on
the window of Merv's Cafe.

"Who will scratch the itch from my back?" he asked.
"*I* will," said Merv. "But first you must
wash my pots and pans."

Shaggy Dog washed towers
and towers of pots and pans.
Bubbles covered his legs and
got into his mouth, and when
he had finished, his paws
were all wrinkly.

Merv used a long fork to
scratch Shaggy Dog's back.
"Ooh, ooh!" said Shaggy Dog.
"That's much, much better."
But when Shaggy Dog left
the cafe . . .

the itch came back!

Shaggy Dog popped into
Mary Lou's Poodle Parlour.

"Will you scratch the itch from my back?"
asked Shaggy Dog.
"Okay," said Mary Lou. "But only if you
brush up the fur on the floor."

Shaggy Dog brushed up
mountains and mountains
of poodle fur.

Fur got up his nose, and when he
had finished, he had fur in his ears
and his eyes, too.

Aitchoo!
Aitchoo!
Aitchoo!

he sneezed.

Shaggy Dog shook out all the fur, and Mary Lou used the poodle brush to scratch his back.

"Ooh, ooh, ooh!" said Shaggy Dog. "That's much, much, MUCH better."

But when Mary Lou stopped scratching . . .

the itch came back!

"What can I do?" asked
Shaggy Dog.
"Sit in the chair," said
Mary Lou. "I'll wash
and trim you."

The bubbly shampoo soothed
Shaggy Dog's back.
"Ooh, ooh, ooh, OOOH!" said
Shaggy Dog.

The
poodle scissors
tickled and went

**Snip! Snip!
Snip!**

"Hee, hee, hee,"
giggled Shaggy
Dog.

When Mary Lou had
finished trimming
Shaggy Dog's fur . . .

Shaggy Dog felt

Wonderful!

The itch had gone at last . . .

but where did it go?

Get the itch for more books from Little Tiger Press

Fireman PiggyWiggy
Christyan and Diane Fox

Wait for me, Little Tiger!
Julie Sykes · Tim Warnes

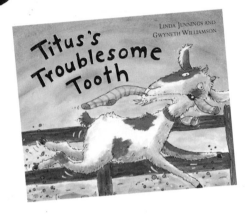

LINDA JENNINGS AND
GWYNETH WILLIAMSON
Titus's Troublesome Tooth

JULIE SYKES · JACK TICKLE
Little Rocket's Special Star

Little Mouse and the Big Red Apple
A.H. Benjamin and Gwyneth Williamson

The Very Noisy Night
Diana Hendry · Jane Chapman

For information regarding any of the above titles or for our catalogue, please contact us at:
Little Tiger Press, 1 The Coda Centre, 189 Munster Road, London SW6 6AW, UK
Tel: 020 7385 6333 • Fax: 020 7385 7333 • E-mail: info@littletiger.co.uk • www.littletigerpress.com